# Zoey AND SASSAFRAS

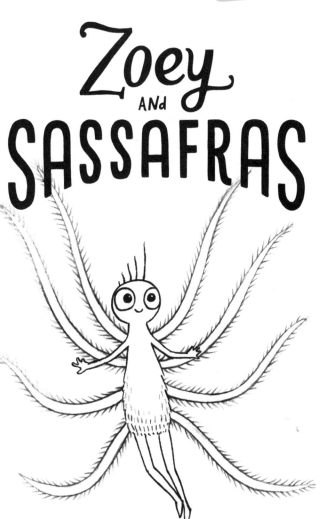

# READ THE REST OF THE SERIES

# TABLE OF CONTENTS

FOR NINA AND TIM, MY PRAWNS! — ML

FOR BUBS AND GOOSE (WITH AN ESPECIALLY BIG THANK YOU TO
TANYA FOR GIVING ME THIS STORY IDEA AND TO MY READERS FOR
HELPING ME BRAINSTORM!) — AC

Audience: Grades K-5.
LCCN 2021938942
ISBN 9781943147946; ISBN 9781943147953; ISBN 9781943147960

Text copyright 2021 by Asia Citro
Illustrations copyright 2021 by Marion Lindsay
Journal entries handwritten by S. Citro

Published by The Innovation Press
7511 Greenwood Ave North #4132, Seattle, WA 98103
*www.theinnovationpress.com*

Printed and bound by Worzalla
Production Date: July 2021 | Plant Location: Stevens Point, Wisconsin

Cover design by Nicole LaRue | Book layout by Kerry Ellis

# PROLOGUE

These days my cat Sassafras and I are always desperately hoping we'll hear our barn doorbell.

I know most people are excited to hear their doorbell ring. It might mean a present or package delivery, or a friend showing up to play. But our doorbell is even more exciting than that. Because it's a *magic* doorbell. When it rings, it means there's a magical animal waiting outside our barn. A magical animal who needs our help.

My mom's been helping them basically her whole life. And now *I* get to help, too . . .

# CHAPTER 1
# SNUGGLEBUGS

"Who is the cutest?" I sang, crouched down low on the floor. "It's you!" I booped one kitten nose. Then I turned. "And it's also you!" I booped a second kitten nose.

One kitten flipped into a half somersault and bopped into her sister. They grabbed each other and started rolling.

I sighed happily. "Is there anything cuter than floofy, tumbly kittens?"

My mom reached down and scooped

one of the fluff balls into her lap. "No, Zoey, I don't think there is!"

We both laughed. "I love volunteering at the cat shelter." Lavender rubbed her cheek against my knee, and I started rubbing her tummy. She flopped to one side, purring loudly.

"Just don't forget that it's a job." Mom nodded toward the litter box.

"I know, I know." I got up and grabbed the scooper. Little Lavender came trotting after me and bonked her head into my ankle.

Mom held up Sage so they faced each other. "Little miss, I just cannot get you to purr." The kitten blinked at her a few times, then curled back up in Mom's lap.

I set down the scooper. "Ooh! I know how to make Sage purr! I figured it out last time we were here. I can show you!"

Mom raised an eyebrow.

I squatted back down and picked up the scooper again. "Um, after I finish scooping the litter."

Mom smiled and pet Sage under the chin. Sage closed her eyes and sighed.

After I closed the lid on the garbage can, I stood up and brushed off my pants. Lavender tumbled into the litter box and sniffed around.

"I think Lavender is making sure I did a good job." I laughed. "OK, so I figured out that Sage is pretty tricky. You can't just do one thing she likes and get her to purr. You have to do two things she likes at the same time!"

Mom nodded. "Interesting. I know she likes these chin rubs—what else do you suggest I try?"

I grinned. "Now go for a belly rub with your other hand."

Mom kept scratching Sage's chin with her right hand and used her left to give that tiny fluffy kitten belly a good rubbing. Sure enough, within a few seconds we both heard a quiet rumbly purr.

"Ta-da!" I raised my hands and smiled.

# CHAPTER 2
# HOME AGAIN

When we got home from the cat shelter, Mom hung up her purse to the sound of galloping kitty paws.

Sassafras skidded to a stop at my feet. "Mrow!"

"Hi, buddy!" I picked him up and tucked his head under my chin.

Sassafras wiggled out from my neck and sniffed me all over. "Mrow?"

"That's just Sage and Lavender you're smelling. They're the kittens at the shelter."

Sassafras jumped down and turned away from me.

I knelt down and ruffled his fur. "Oh, Sass, you're still my favorite. Besides, the kittens have a loving home all set up. They just need another week to get bigger and stronger at the shelter before they go."

Sassafras glanced back at me and then licked his toes.

Mom laughed. "I think someone's feeling a little jealous."

I tapped a finger to my lip. "I know just the thing to make it up to him!"

I strolled into the kitchen and opened a can of tuna. Sassafras came running so quickly he slid into my legs.

"Here you go, buddy. Sorry I smell like kittens!" I said as I set down the can of tuna on the ground. I expected to see Sassafras's happy face staring back at me . . . but there was no Sassafras.

"Sassafras?" I looked around the kitchen and under the table. Then I spun around just in time to see the cat door flapping.

Wow, he must really be upset with me to turn down a fresh can of tuna! But then it all made sense. Because I heard what Sassafras must've heard over the sound of the can opener—the magic doorbell!

# CHAPTER 3
# IT'S NOT FUNNY

Sassafras was already meowing at the back barn door by the time I got there. I took a quick moment to close my eyes and hope for an exciting new magical creature to help. Then I slowly opened the door . . . and immediately doubled over laughing. Oh my goodness.

"It's not funny." Pip stood outside the barn door with his arms crossed. And with a full head of flowing green curly hair.

Sassafras meowed and leapt backward,

which only made me laugh harder.

I swallowed hard. "I'm so sorry, Pip."

Pip rolled his eyes. "I am sure it looks somewhat silly, but–"

"Oh my. You haven't seen it yet?" I choked out. It was very hard to hold back my laughter.

Pip shook his head, which made the

green curls bounce. He took one of the longer locks of hair and held it in front of his face. "I mean, I can see parts of it, obviously."

I held up a finger (it was easier to not laugh if I didn't talk) and turned to look through the drawers in the barn. "Bingo!" I whispered and held up a small mirror. I swallowed hard to keep myself calm, walked back to Pip, and showed him.

"OH! Oh my!" Pip exclaimed. And then began to giggle. He bent over laughing hard, and I joined in. "OK, OK, I guess it is pretty funny for a frog to have hair." He poofed up each side with a hand. "But the green looks good with my purple skin!"

I smiled and nodded. "Is it a wig?"

"Nope, it's real hair!" Pip shrugged.

I wrinkled my eyebrows together. "But . . . ?"

"I know. I don't get it, either. I was walking through the forest when the top of my head began tingling. I started scratching and *poof*—all of a sudden I had hair!" Pip looked down at the ground and blushed. "I maybe might have screamed at that point." He moved some dirt around with his foot. "I maybe might have screamed most of the way here."

I wiped my eyes and bent down. "Oh, Pip. I am sure it was pretty scary. I honestly don't know what I would do if I was walking alone in the woods and suddenly sprouted very colorful new hair."

Pip gave me a little smile. He reached up and grabbed two handfuls of green curls and gave them a tug. "It definitely does not come off. But, uh, I'd prefer to not live the rest of my life with hair, so . . . do you think you can fix it?"

"Hmmmm." I sat down cross-legged next to my friend. "How to fix a case of sudden hair. Ummm." I looked over at Pip and his eyes got a little watery. I gulped and straightened my back. "We'll sort it out, Pip. Don't worry!"

# CHAPTER 4

# RETRACE

# YOUR STEPS

"OK, first things first." I folded my hands in my lap. "Let's retrace your steps."

Pip looked at me with an open mouth for a moment. "Um, trace my feet? How will that help with my hair?"

I smiled. "It means go back to where you were when it happened. It's something my parents make me do if I've lost something. You can do it in your mind, too. Just think back in your memory and tell me everything you were doing right before your hair, um, sprouted."

"Ohhhh," said Pip. He twisted his mouth to one side and looked up. "Let's see. I was walking through the trees by the merhorse stream."

"Were you touching anything?"

"Nope."

"Huh. OK, um, did you hear anything or see anything unusual?"

"Nope."

"OK, so you were just walking normally, not touching anything, not hearing or seeing anything unusual, and the next thing you knew your head was kind of itchy and then the hair appeared?"

"Exactly!" said Pip.

He sat down cross-legged next to me and put a hand on his chin just like me. Sassafras joined us, and we all sat there in silence.

"Hmmm . . ." I said. "I guess let's go look in person? Maybe we'll notice something you didn't?"

Pip stood up and nodded, which made his curls bounce. "I think that's a good idea!"

"To the forest we go!" I cheered.

# CHAPTER 5

# SHOUTING

Pip waved his hand back and forth. "I was right about here when it happened."

I looked around—nothing.

I bent down and looked closely at the ground and the plants—nothing.

I listened quietly—nothing.

What was I going to tell Pip? How was I going to fix this for him?

"Mrow?" Sassafras pointed his ears over to a section of the forest farther away.

"Do you hear something, buddy?"

I strained my ears, and I still didn't hear anything. But Sassafras blinked up at me once and took off through the forest.

"Hey, wait for us!" I called. I jogged after my cat, and Pip hopped alongside me, green curls bouncing. "WHOAAAAA!" I turned around a tree and almost ran into two forest monsters who were having a big fight.

"UGHHH, stop touching me!" shouted the girl monster.

"YOUUUU stop touching me!" the boy monster shouted back.

"AAAAGHHH!" they both screamed as Sassafras skidded to a stop at their feet.

I dashed forward and scooped up a loudly purring Sass.

"Sorry about my cat." I held my squirmy Sassafras just a little tighter. "I'll make sure he stays over here. Is everything OK?"

The two monsters shook their heads no at the same time.

"I was just playing with my brother," said the girl monster.

"Yeah, and then she wouldn't stop grabbing my hand," said the brother.

"No, you wouldn't stop grabbing *my* hand!" said the sister.

I plopped Sassafras down and wagged a finger at him. "You stay here!" Then I turned to the monsters. "Can I take a closer look at your hands?"

They nodded at the same time. "What happens when you try to pull them apart?"

They pulled back a little and I bent over and looked really closely. It kind of looked like gum or glue was in there because their hands wouldn't come apart at all. "Are you sure you didn't touch anything? Like a strange plant? Neither of you was chewing gum or anything like that?"

They shook their heads.

This was definitely weird. "My mom might know a way to get your hands

unstuck. Do you want to come back to my house?"

"Yes, please!" said the girl monster. The boy monster nodded.

As the group of us walked back toward my house, my mind was spinning. Was Pip's hair related to these stuck hands? Were two different things going wrong? What was happening in our forest!?

# CHAPTER 6
# TINY!

We had only taken a few steps toward home when Pip stopped and put a hand down to the ground. "Do you feel that?"

I held very still. Nope. Nothing.

Sassafras, however, froze for a moment, and then bolted off into the forest once more.

"Not again!" I grumbled.

Pip hopped onto my head and settled in cross-legged. "I'll let you do the running this time," he chuckled.

I took a deep breath and set off again after that Sassafras!

This time Sassafras had gone much farther, and I was busy trying to spot him in the tall grass when I almost ran into a furry white tree trunk. Wait. *Wait!* That wasn't a tree trunk!

"TINY!!!!!!!!!!!!" I squealed and wrapped my arms around the leg of my favorite baby unicorn.

"ZOEY! CAT! FROG! MONSTERS!" Tiny happily bobbed his head up and down.

The wind from Tiny's giant head nodding knocked all of us over.

I stood up laughing and took a bunch of steps back, just in case Tiny nodded again. Pip and the monsters joined me, but Sassafras insisted on rubbing and purring all over Tiny's giant legs.

"FROG NEW HAIR?"

"Well, yes," Pip answered. "But not on purpose . . ."

"Pip was walking along when this hair just popped up on his head. Have you seen anything strange like that happening in the forest?" I asked.

Tiny opened his mouth to answer, but instead of words, bubbles came out.

"Whoa," Pip said and stumbled backward.

"Tiny?" I asked.

Then all of a sudden Tiny's fur changed

from white to zebra stripes.

Sassafras puffed up and ran back to me. He hid behind my legs.

The monsters screamed.

One last bubble popped out of Tiny's mouth. "WHY TINY CHANGING?"

Oh no. Not another change! I looked all around and didn't see anything that could be causing it, but Sassafras's ears flicked to the side.

I heard a quiet kind of tapping noise somewhere in the distance. I turned to ask Tiny what that sound was when all of a sudden–*poof.* Tiny was gone.

"TINY!" I screamed.

Pip fainted.

The monsters ran off to hide.

Sassafras yowled and leapt forward to where Tiny had been just a few moments before.

"NOOOOOOOOO!!!!" I sank down to my knees and sobbed.

"Meow!" said Sassafras as he pawed at

the ground.

I started to cry. Oh, how could Tiny be *gone*?

"MEOW!" said Sassafras again.

"Maybe he disappeared here and reappeared somewhere else in the forest?" I said, trying to calm myself down. "Or maybe–"

"MEOWWW!" said Sassafras even more loudly.

Oh! I rushed over to Sassafras and knelt down beside him. "Oh my goodness!" I gasped. "Is that . . . ???"

"Meow," said Sassafras quietly as he bent down to give a nose boop to a very, very tiny Tiny!

# CHAPTER 7
# WHAT IS HAPPENING?!

I laid down my hand, and the tiny Tiny jumped up into my palm. I held him close to my face. "Tiny? Is that you?"

"Zoey! Why?" asked a teeny-tiny Tiny voice.

"Oh, friend. I wish I knew." I swallowed hard. "I think something weird is happening in the forest, but I don't know what. I'm taking you back to our barn for now. I think you'll be safe there."

Tiny nodded his tiny head. Oh, how I

missed the big gusts of wind his normal head nods made.

I scooped up poor unconscious Pip in my other hand, and called the scared monster siblings over. Once we had gathered everyone, Sassafras and I carefully took our friends back toward home.

When we were inside the warm barn, Pip sat up and rubbed his face. Then he put a hand over his mouth and looked up at me with big eyes. "Tiny? He's . . . gone?"

I pointed to a tray I'd set next to Pip on the barn table. "Thankfully, no. He's just tiny."

Pip and the monsters walked over and peered into the tray. "Oh, thank goodness!" Pip said and reached out to pet our tiny unicorn friend. Then he looked up at me. "Zoey, what is going on?!"

I opened my mouth to answer when the magic doorbell rang.

The monster brother and sister, who

had been peeking at tiny Tiny, ran to a corner and hid under a blanket.

Pip and I looked at each other and rushed over to where Sassafras was waiting by the door. It must be another magical creature who was affected by . . . whatever this was.

I opened the door to see a poofy creature who was floating. And crying. And making a familiar noise.

"Hey, I know that sound!" I said.

"Are you–*hic*–Zoey? I . . ." said the
creature.

"EEEEEEEEEKKK!" said Pip. "Zoey!"
I turned to Pip and yelped.

# CHAPTER 8
## PIP?

Where my friend Pip had been just a moment before, there was now a furry blue . . . thing? "Aaaghh!" I yelped again.

"Zoey, it's me!" said the furry thing.

Sassafras was all poofed out, carefully sniffing the blue creature. I rubbed my eyes. Oh! It was Pip. His green hair was gone. And instead of Pip's purple and neon orange polka-dotted frog skin, he was now covered in fluffy blue fur.

"Oh no—*hic*—oh no—*hic*—not again—

*hic*–!" said the floating creature who had rung the magic doorbell.

"Ack!" said Pip.

My head bounced back and forth between the creature and Pip. Pip was now his normal color, with no fur or hair–but he had just laid a chicken egg.

As the egg slowly rolled to a stop by his paw, Sassafras bolted and hid behind a stack of books.

"Oh my!" I said to Pip, and I then I spun back to the floating creature. "Ummmm, sorry—one moment!"

I shut the barn door and rushed Pip back over to Tiny. Was he changing, too? What if he got even tinier?

"Pheww," I said. Tiny was unchanged. "Well, I think we found out what has been causing all the changes in the forest."

Pip shivered and looked at his arms and legs, which were back to normal . . . for now. "Ohhh!" he said. "That makes sense."

I shook my head. What was he talking about? Nothing was making sense!

Pip put his hand on mine. "That was a Wishypoof, Zoey."

"A whaaa–?" I said.

"Ah, you probably haven't seen one before. They are pretty rare. Wishypoofs are magical creatures that can grant wishes!"

I shook my head again. "But—you didn't wish to lay an egg . . . did you?"

Pip stuck out his tongue. "Oh, goodness no!"

I thought for a moment. That sound . . . she had the hiccups! "Do you think maybe her magic is not working right because she's hiccupping?"

Pip put a hand to his chin and thought for a moment. "Maybe! We should go ask her!" He stood up and then froze. "Um, maybe *you* should go ask her. It seems safer for me to stay here."

I nodded and hurried back to the barn door. Just as I was about to open it, I paused. The last time I opened the door, Pip turned into a fluffy blue frog. I went around the long way just to be safe.

Once I reached the back of the barn I could hear the *hic—hic—hic* sound of hiccups.

"Um, hello? Wishypoof?"

She slowly floated over to me and dried her eyes. "Are you–*hic*–Zoey?"

"That's me! Are you doing OK?"

"Not really–*hic*–" Tears ran down her tiny face. "I don't–*hic*–know what–*hic*–is going on–*hic*–but I started–*hic*–making this weird–*hic*–noise and then–*hic*–my wishing powers–*hic*–started changing the–*hic*–forest creatures–*hic*–" She had to stop talking for a moment because she was crying too hard.

"Oh, don't worry . . . um, Miss Wishypoof. We'll find a way to fix it!" I gently patted her.

"You can–*hic*–call me–*hic*–Wishy." She brushed away her tears.

"I–*hic*–think I–*hic*–keep changing–*hic*–forest creatures–*hic*–and . . . and–*hic*–and I–*hic*–think I–*hic*–just made–*hic*–a baby unicorn–*hic*–DISAPPEAAAR!" she wailed.

"Oh! No–Tiny isn't gone. He's just . . . tiny. I have him in the barn right now," I told her.

"Really?" She sniffed. "He's–*hic*–safe?" I nodded.

"I don't–*hic*–want to–*hic*–keep doing–*hic*–this–*hic*–" She wiped her nose. "Can you–*hic*–make this–*hic*–go away?"

"I think you just have the hiccups," I said.

"The–*hic*–what?" she asked.

"Hiccups. You know? When your stomach kind of squinches up and you make that sound?"

She wrinkled up her face. "I have—*hic*—never heard of—*hic*—hiccups. They must—*hic*—be what—*hic*—is making—*hic*—my magic—*hic*—do these—*hic*—weird things—*hic*. How do—*hic*—you make them—*hic*—go away?"

"Well . . . that's a good question. In my family we hold our breath for as long as we can."

Wishy nodded and closed her mouth.

Her little cheeks puffed out, and her face turned red. I could still hear little hiccups as she did it, but I crossed my fingers that this would work.

"*Ptttfffff!*" She let out her breath. "I–*hic*–couldn't hold–*hic*–my breath–*hic*–any longer–*hic*. Oh no–*hic*–I am–*hic*–still–hiccupping!"

"Hmmm. OK, we'll try something else. But I'm not sure what . . . yet. Are you OK waiting here in the backyard?"

She nodded and hiccupped quietly.

"OK, you stay here," I said. "I'll make sure Pip and Tiny didn't change again, and then I'll go ask my mom about it. She's a scientist. She'll totally be able to help us." I gave Wishy what I hoped was a confident grin.

# CHAPTER 9
# WHAT ARE HICCUPS?

"So, Pip and Tiny seem safe from any more unexpected changes in the barn?" Mom asked.

I nodded. "I think the hiccups are making Wishy's magic go all wonky. So we just need to cure her hiccups. That should be easy, right?" I looked hopefully at Mom.

"Well . . . they can sometimes be a bit tricky," Mom said. "There's not really a proven cure."

"Great." I flopped my head on the table,

then turned it to the side to look at Mom. "What even are hiccups? And why can't you just *decide* to stop hiccupping?"

"Those are excellent questions," Mom said with a twinkle in her eye. "I could tell you, but I'd rather show you."

I perked up. "Show me?"

Mom smiled. "You go find a plastic bottle from the recycling and grab two balloons and some tape. I'll get the scissors."

I grabbed the supplies and brought them to the table. "This part is tricky," Mom said, using the scissors to cut the bottle in half, "so an adult needs to do it."

She set the bottom half of the bottle aside and passed the top half and the scissors to me. "Now it's your turn," she continued. "Squeeze one of the balloons through the mouth of the bottle—that's the top part you drink from. Good. Now stretch the opening of the balloon over the mouth of the bottle."

She handed me the other balloon and had me cut the skinny part off. Then I stretched the remaining part of the balloon over the open bottom of the bottle and taped it in place.

I held up the finished product. One balloon dangled down inside from where it was stretched over the mouth of the bottle, and the other covered the entire bottom part of the bottle.

"This is a pretty simple model of your lungs. You really have two lungs, of course, but for this we'll pretend like you have one." She pointed to the whole balloon

hanging from the top of the bottle. "This balloon is your lung." She tapped the plastic bottle. "This is your rib cage." And then she tapped the stretched-out balloon on the bottom of the bottle. "And this is your diaphragm."

I raised an eyebrow. "Diaphragm?"

Mom pointed to a place on her stomach above her belly button. "Your diaphragm is a big muscle at the bottom of your rib cage that you use without thinking to breathe," she said. "OK, now pinch the center part of the lower balloon and pull it down."

"WHOA!" I shouted. "When I pull that down, the lung balloon blows up!"

"That's how you breathe in," said Mom. "When you tighten your diaphragm, it pulls down and your lungs inflate with air. Now push the diaphragm balloon up."

"Whoa!" I said again. "So when my diaphragm goes up, my lungs breathe out?"

"You've got it!" Mom said.

I paused. "But what does this have to do with hiccups?"

"Aha, good question. Make the diaphragm move up and down really quickly."

I did, and the lung balloon started looking a bit wonky.

"Remember how I said you don't think about breathing—you just do it? Well, that's because your brain sends a message

to your diaphragm to move. But if your brain sends weird signals, it makes your diaphragm all jumpy. That's part of what makes you feel uncomfortable. But it also makes you breathe out faster than normal, and when you do that, your vocal cords close and make a *hic* sound."

"Ohhhhhh," I said. "And no one really knows how to make your brain stop sending weird signals to your diaphragm to make the hiccups stop?"

Mom nodded. "Every family kind of has their own cure, but there's not one thing that always works. Like we have you hold your breath, right? And it sometimes works, but sometimes not."

I sat up straighter. "So . . . other families might have different ideas to try?"

"Mm-hmm. Why are you smiling?" Mom asked.

"Because I've got a plan! Thanks, Mom!" I grabbed the lung model and dashed out the door.

# CHAPTER 10
# CAN I COME, TOO?

"I think we should ask different magical creatures what they do for hiccups. Wishy is magical, so it makes sense to try things that work for other magical creatures. Don't you think?" I asked Pip, but he didn't respond. "Pip? PIP!"

"Oh, sorry," Pip said, finally looking up. "It's just really fun to make this lung blow up." He pulled down on the bottom diaphragm balloon one last time, and then sighed and handed back the lung model. "But yes, I think that is a great plan."

"Excellent! You wait here, and I'll go tell Wishy. It's probably best if she stays here so we don't have any more wacky changes to the forest creatures." I grabbed the lung model, but Pip looked up at me with big eyes. "OK, fine. You can play with the lung model while I go talk to her," I said. Pip hopped up and down and reached his arms out for it.

I checked in on the monster siblings, who preferred to stay snuggled up in their corner of the barn. Then I came out around the barn and heard Wishy crying. "Are you doing OK?" I asked gently.

Wishy took a big sniff. "I'm just—*hic*—so lonely—*hic*. I came—*hic*—to the forest—*hic*—to make—*hic*—some new—*hic*—friends, but—*hic*—I have—*hic*—just made—*hic*—a mess—*hic*—of everything."

"It was an accident, though. And don't worry—we're going to fix it!" I told her my plan to ask around in the forest.

She wiped her eyes and smiled. "Can I–*hic*–come, too–*hic*–? I mean–*hic*–if we–*hic*–can find–*hic*–some way–*hic*–for me to–*hic*–not accidentally–*hic*–cause problems?"

I thought for a minute. It would be safer to leave her here . . .

Wishy looked at my face and started crying again. "Please don't–*hic*–leave me–*hic*–here. I–*hic*–am so–*hic*–lonely!"

I rolled my shoulders. There must be some way to make this work. "OK, let's see. You're not causing Pip or Tiny to change right now, which is good. But you were causing them to change earlier in the forest and when Pip was standing at the barn door. So something we were doing then made the magic work, and something we're doing now has stopped it. Were you looking at Pip and Tiny earlier when they changed?"

Wishy thought for a minute. "I—*hic*—think so—*hic*—"

"OK, I have an idea. Wait here!" I dashed into the barn and found a small piece of cloth. I held it up to my eye. "This will make a perfect blindfold!"

I walked over to Pip. "I'm so sorry to have to ask, but Wishy wants to come with us, and I need to figure out why her magic isn't changing you—right now, anyway. I think if she looks at a magical creature while she hiccups, that's when the accidental magic happens." I showed Pip the little blindfold cloth.

"Meep!" he said. He stepped to the side and pointed at a newly laid chicken egg. "I'll help you test her magic. Even if the blindfold doesn't work, I might stop laying chicken eggs."

"OK, you wait at the back barn door. I'll go put the blindfold on Wishy, open the door, and you can come out. If nothing about you changes, we'll know the

blindfold stops her magic."

I went around the side of the barn to
Wishy and explained the plan. Once she
was blindfolded, I opened the barn door
and Pip stepped out and stood next to her,
just as she hiccupped.

"Oh dear," Pip said.

I looked down at my frog friend, who
was no longer laying chicken eggs . . . but
who now had feet as long as his arms.
He looked like he was wearing giant
swimming flippers!

"Ack!" I scooped him up, plopped him

into the barn, and shut the door.

"Did I—*hic*—do it—*hic*—again?" Wishy began to wail.

"Well, yes . . . but it wasn't your fault!" I patted Wishy. "OK, so the unwanted changes must not be caused by you looking at them. What else could it be?" I tapped my head. Oh! I needed my trusty Thinking Goggles! "One sec!" I told Wishy as I ran off to grab them.

Once I got my goggles, I made sure they were nice and snug on top of my head and thought over everything I knew about when Wishy's magic did or didn't change my friends.

"OK, Thinking Goggles . . ." I muttered.

I closed my eyes tight, and a memory of Tiny popped into my head—first the bubbles, and then zebra stripes, and then shrinking . . . while Pip, Sass, the monsters, and I watched from across the field. "THAT'S IT!" I shouted.

"What's—*hic*—what?" Wishy asked.

"In the forest when Tiny was changing, Pip and the monsters were farther away from you and not changing. Right now, they are in the barn, which is also farther away from you. I think if we can make sure you stay a good distance away from any other magical creatures, you won't accidentally change them."

I looked from Wishy to the barn, and then I took four big steps back from the barn door and waved her over. "You stay over here, OK?"

Wishy nodded and quietly hiccupped.

I opened the barn door and peeked my head in. "Are you OK, Pip?"

Pip marched over with his giant feet and grinned. "I still just have my big old feet. Nothing else changed!"

"I think it's distance that makes Wishy's magic work or not work," I said. "Are you OK with me trying again?"

"Hmm . . . I do kind of like these giant feet because—watch this!" Pip jumped super-duper high.

"WHOA!" I exclaimed.

"They're cool, right?" He grinned. "But sure, we can try again."

"In that case, here we goooo . . ." I said, and then slowly opened the door.

My head bounced from Wishy to Pip's giant feet and back again.

I waited a full minute to be sure. "I think . . ."

"We did it!" Pip cheered and gave another giant leap.

# CHAPTER 11
# LET'S FIND
# A CURE

I breathed a sigh of relief at having figured something out. "Let's get down to business. Which magical creatures should we ask about hiccup cures first?" I asked Pip.

Pip blinked at me.

"What?" I raised an eyebrow.

He crossed his arms. "Seriously, Zoey?"

"What am I missing?"

"Ummm, you're talking to a magical creature right now! Aren't you going to ask *me*?" Pip humphed.

"Oh goodness—of course! I am so sorry. Pip, how does your family cure hiccups?" I asked.

"We drink a big cup of water all through a straw," Pip answered proudly.

"You guys have straws?" I asked.

"Of course we have straws." Pip frowned. "Why wouldn't we have straws?"

I shrugged. "We have metal straws, but they're people-sized. They'd be too big for Wishy."

Pip nodded. "Come with me." He marched with his giant feet out into the backyard, but kept a careful eye on Wishy to make sure he didn't get too close. He picked a dandelion, plucked the flower off, and handed me the stem. "Ta-da!"

I held it, and then grinned at a memory. "Oh, of course they make perfect straws! In the summer we use dandelion stems to blow bubbles in the backyard. Thank you, Pip!" I reached down and gave him a high-five.

Next, I went in the barn and found a little cap that would work as a small cup and filled it with water from the sink. Along the way I peered behind a stack of books where Sassafras was tucked away.

"Oh, buddy!" I reached down and ruffled his fur. "I think it's OK to come out now. We figured out how to make Pip stop changing. Plus you should see his new

feet!"

Sassafras popped his head up, sniffed a bit, and then hopped out and marched off like he'd never been scared in the first place.

I giggled and followed him back over to Pip.

We had Pip wait a good distance away, and then took the water and straw over and handed them to Wishy.

"Pip's family hiccup cure is drinking a full glass of water through a straw, so let's try that first."

We all watched as she carefully drank the full cup of water through the dandelion stem straw.

Pip clasped his hands. "Did it work?"

A tear rolled down Wishy's cheek. "I don't think it–*hic*–worked."

My Thinking Goggles got a little tight. "What am I missing?" I asked myself. I walked in a little circle. "Oh! Can you say something else, Wishy?"

"What do you want–*hic*–me to say?"

I grinned. "Did you hear that?"

"Mrow!" said Sassafras.

"Oh yeahhh!" said Pip. "She's hiccupping a little less, right?"

I nodded. "I'll have to track this. I need to get my science journal!"

# CHAPTER 12

# DATA

"That's more like it," I said when I finished writing in my science journal.

Pip looked over my shoulder at the data chart. "So we need to retry the first two fixes?"

"Exactly. This time I've got a chart and a stopwatch so we can actually measure whether the cures work or not—and how well."

Sassafras purred.

We retested having Wishy hold her

breath and drink a cup of water through a straw, and I added the data to my chart:

| CURE | Hiccups per minute BEFORE | Hiccups per minute AFTER |
|---|---|---|
| Hold your breath as long as possible | 38 | 45 |
| Drink a cup of water through a straw | 46 | 31 |

I closed my science journal and went back into the barn. I knelt down and whispered to tiny Tiny, "How do unicorns cure hiccups?"

Tiny shook his little head. "What is hiccup?" I explained with my lung model, but Tiny still shook his head. "Unicorns no hiccup."

I sighed and walked around the barn until I found the monster siblings' hiding spot.

"I think it's safe for you guys to come out now. As long as you don't get close to Wishy, you should be fine. She's outside so you could totally hang out in the barn if you want."

They shook their heads no. "Umm, we'd rather stay over here if that's OK," said the girl.

The boy monster shivered. "I do *not* want to end up laying chicken eggs."

I shrugged. Then I asked, "How do you guys cure hiccups?"

"We hold our breath!" they said at the same time.

"OK, thanks," I said, trying not to sound disappointed.

I walked back outside. "Unicorns don't get hiccups, and monsters seem to use the same cure my family does. Which means we have one hiccup fix that kind of works, and one that definitely doesn't," I said. "Should we ask around in the forest and see if other magical creatures have new things for us to try?"

Pip and Wishy nodded, and Sassafras meowed.

As we walked through the forest, Wishy was careful to stay several feet away from Pip, who marched by my side with his enormous feet.

Suddenly Pip stopped. "Do you hear that?"

"Is that . . . someone laughing?" I asked.

Pip smiled. "Yep. I bet those are chortles! Let's go find out."

We all followed Pip, and the sound of laughter got louder and louder. I soon spotted a group of six creatures that looked a bit like a goat and a fox mixed together. But smaller, and with eight legs each! Even though I was worried about poor Wishy, I couldn't help but feel a little burst of excitement at being introduced to a new kind of magical creature.

"Hello there!" Pip called, while I quietly timed and counted Wishy's hiccups and added that information to my chart. "Our friend Wishy has a bad case of hiccups, and it's making her magic do silly things." Pip paused and held up one of his giant feet and wiggled it, and the chortles giggled. "We were wondering how you get rid of hiccups?"

The chortles looked at each other and laughed. The one on the far left said, "Well, first you put one finger on your nose."

Wishy, who was still a good distance away, put one finger on her nose.

Another chortle said, "Then you put your other hand on your hip."

Wishy did that as well.

The next chortle said, "Then you flap your elbows."

Another added, "Don't forget to hop on one foot!"

A fifth chortle said, "And you have to do all that while you spin around."

The last chortle looked at our group. "It works best if you all do it at the same time."

Pip, Wishy, and I did our best to follow all of those directions while Sassafras just galloped in circles. Then Pip tripped over Sassafras and they landed in a pile, which made me start laughing, and I tripped over a small branch and fell, too.

The whole group of us, even Wishy,

couldn't stop laughing for a full minute.

Pip wiped laughing tears away from his eyes. "Is that really what you do every time you get the hiccups?" he asked the chortles.

"Well . . . not really," said one.

"We do cure them by laughing, though," said another.

"Because laughter is the best medicine!" squeaked the smallest.

"Phewww." I grabbed my stomach, now exhausted from giggling. "Let's see if that worked." I pulled out my stopwatch and timed Wishy's hiccups. I shook my head sadly.

Wishy took a shaky breath. "Thank–*hic*–you for–*hic*–trying."

Oh no. Poor Wishy. There had to be a way to fix this! I stood up straighter and squinched my eyes up tight. "Oh! Let's go ask the caterflies next! They're small and they fly just like you. Maybe they will know just what to do!"

# CHAPTER 13
# CATERFLIES

"Mrow!" called Sassafras as we turned the corner to the little meadow where the caterflies lived.

I looked down to see a caterfly riding on Sassafras's head. I bent closer and heard the unmistakable tiny purr of a happy caterfly.

"Hello, sweet little friend!" I said, and before I knew it, about a dozen caterflies were hovering around us. One landed on Pip's head, one landed on my shoulder, and two caterflies flew over to Wishy.

"WAIT!" she shouted. "Don't come–
*hic*–any closer!"

The two caterflies looked from Wishy to me and back again.

I held out a hand, and they landed. "Our friend Wishy has a bad case of hiccups, and they make her magic do strange things. If you don't get too close to her, you should be safe."

Pip called out, "We are asking everyone for their hiccup cures to try to help Wishy."

One of the caterflies in my hand said, "Ahhh. In that case, wait here, please!"

She meowed once, and five other caterflies flew off with her.

I raised an eyebrow at Pip. He shrugged and reached up to pet the caterfly under the chin.

They were only gone a minute. I pointed to six caterflies carrying a large yellow thing between them. "Pip? Is that a . . . lemon?"

Pip squinted. "I think it is!"

The group of caterflies flew to my hand.

"Oof! Here you go, Zoey! If you peel that and have your friend suck on it, that should fix her hiccups," the caterfly said proudly.

"Wait here with Pip and Sassafras," I told the caterflies.

"Oooooooh, Sassafras!" half a dozen tiny caterfly voices squealed as they burrowed into my cat's fur.

I peeled the lemon and handed it to Wishy. Then I pulled out my stopwatch to time her hiccups and gave her the thumbs-up. Wishy took the lemon in both hands and took a big bite. She sucked in the lemon juice, and her face wrinkled up.

"Oh, wow—*hic*—that is—*hic*—really so—*hic*—very sour—*hic*—!"

I lowered my stopwatch and shook my head. "The lemon juice made it worse."

"Oh no!" cried a caterfly.

"We're so sorry," said another.

"Something sour always seems to work when we get the hiccups," said the caterfly that had been on my hand.

"Don't worry about it!" I said. "There's really no single cure for the hiccups. That's why we're asking everyone. Even though it didn't work, you gave us some good information. Now we know lemons won't cure Wishy."

Pip added, "Thank you so much for trying, caterflies!"

We waved goodbye, and all the caterflies swarmed Sassafras once more for a big snuggle before we left.

"Hippogriffs next?" suggested Pip, and I nodded.

# CHAPTER 14

# HIPPOGRIFFS

"Erm, you should probably wait here," Pip said.

I sat cross-legged at the base of the rocks where the hippogriffs nested, and Sassafras curled up in my lap. Wishy waited until Pip was far enough away and then floated over to me and Sass.

Pip handled the tricky climb up easily with his large feet gripping the rocks. "Excuse me, sir and ma'am?" Pip called.

We heard two loud eagle screeches as

the hippogriffs answered Pip, who then explained our situation. "So, if you have any good hiccup cures . . ."

The hippogriffs screeched again. One of them stood and tucked its head down by its talons and then bobbed its head. It screeched one last time.

"We will give that a try! Thank you so much!" Pip tromped back over to us. "Do you still have that cup and some water?" Pip asked me. I pulled out the small cup and water bottle from my backpack. "Excellent." Pip turned so he also faced Wishy far behind us. "They said to take a cup full of water, bend over, and drink it while you're upside down."

I poured the Wishy-sized cup of water and gave it to her. After I timed her hiccups yet again, Wishy bent over and did her best to drink from the cup upside down. She straightened up and brushed a drop of water from her forehead.

"That was—*hic*—pretty tricky—*hic*—"

I sat with my timer for a minute, then sighed. "Well . . . it didn't make the hiccups worse. But it didn't make them better, either."

Pip put his hand on mine. "Don't worry, Zoey. I'm sure we'll figure it out . . . eventually."

I thought of poor tiny Tiny back at the barn, and my stomach felt heavy. "I hope so, Pip." I looked around. "We're kind of by Gorp's house. Should we at least check with him?"

# CHAPTER 15
# PEANUT BUTTER

Gorp answered after Pip's third knock on his door. "Zoey! Pip!" Our forest monster friend hugged us both. "Ohh . . . and Sassafras, too," he added nervously.

He gulped and held out a hand, squinting while Sassafras purred and rubbed against it. Seeing how uncomfortable he was, I scooped up a wiggly Sassafras.

We explained the whole story. "As my

family says, a spoonful of peanut butter a day keeps the hiccups away!" Gorp went back inside his house and returned holding a toothpick full of peanut butter. "I figured a spoon would be too big, but this should do the trick!"

I recorded Wishy's hiccup timing in my journal, and then gave her the toothpick of peanut butter.

"I just—*hic*—eat the—*hic*—whole thing—*hic*—?"

Gorp folded his arms proudly. "Exactly."

Wishy stuck the glob of peanut butter into her mouth. She swallowed a few times. "That was really good—*hic*—peanut butter. Thank you, Gorp—*hic*—!"

Pip and I looked at each other. I grabbed my stopwatch to be sure. Then I gave Gorp a big hug. "Thank you, Gorp!" I showed him my data chart. "The peanut butter helped a lot!"

I let out a big breath. We were finally getting closer to fixing this!

# CHAPTER 16
# NOW WHAT?

Three hours later I dramatically dropped down to the forest floor with my arms and legs spread out. I stared up at the sky and blew out a giant breath. "Now what?" I asked Pip.

Pip opened his mouth to answer. Then closed it again.

Sassafras booped my cheek to make me feel better.

I sighed. "I really thought we were getting closer after talking to Gorp and trying the peanut butter, but the last four groups of creatures we asked had the same ideas we've already tried."

"I know," said Pip. "I'm really not sure what to try next."

"And it's getting late." I sighed again. "I really need to head home."

"Oh," Wishy whispered. She started crying quietly.

I sat up. "I'm so sorry, Wishy. When we get home, I'll ask my mom for any other ideas she might have."

We slowly made our way back home. I had Pip go check on Tiny and the monster siblings. I went into the house to talk with Mom while Wishy waited outside the barn. I flumped down at the kitchen table and laid my head on my arms.

Mom came over and rubbed my back. "It's going that well, huh?"

I turned my head to the side. "I feel like we asked everyone in the forest today. Two things almost worked, but not all the way. Everything else either did nothing or made the hiccups worse." I pulled out my science journal to show my mom all the things we'd tried.

"Well, it does look like you've tried everything I've heard of. And even some things I hadn't." Mom sat down next to me at the table. "Isn't it funny how the magical creatures cures are similar to human cures?"

I nodded. "I noticed that, too."

Mom thought for a minute. "Well, with humans, sometimes it just takes time for hiccups to go away. Maybe that will work for Wishy, too! Why don't you make everyone comfortable for the night, and perhaps she will be better in the morning?"

"OK," I grumbled. "I guess we haven't tried leaving the hiccups alone yet."

I walked back out to the barn and laid a little folded-up tissue in the tray with Tiny so he'd have somewhere cozy to sleep. Pip

decided to go home for the night.

I took Wishy over to our greenhouse. "It should be warmer in here tonight. I hope those pesky hiccups go away while you sleep!"

She hugged me. "Thank you for–*hic*–trying so hard–*hic*–Zoey."

As I went inside for the night, I tried to be hopeful that the hiccups would finally be gone by the morning.

# CHAPTER 17
# OH NO!

The next morning, Sassafras and I rushed through breakfast, grabbed a sweater, and bolted to the greenhouse to check on Wishy.

As we ran, I whispered, "Please be gone, hiccups, please be gone!"

I threw open the greenhouse door, and Wishy rubbed her eyes. "Good morning, Zoey—*hic*. How did you sleep—*hic*—?" And then she started to cry. "I still—*hic*—have the—*hic*—cups!"

I felt like I'd swallowed a rock. We'd tried everything we could think of. And even waiting didn't work. What were we going to do now? I could feel tears starting to come, but I didn't want Wishy to lose hope. "Well, we just have to think of more things to try, right?"

Wishy nodded sadly. She floated past me over to the tree beside the barn. I tried to think while I watched Sassafras roll around in the grass. None of us were paying attention when Pip came bounding back to the barn through the forest.

"Hey, Zoey, did—" Pip started to say right behind me.

And Wishy was right in front of me.

I spun around—Pip was too close! I tried to push him away, but I wasn't fast enough—*poof*! Pip turned into a tadpole right before my eyes.

He landed on the grass and wiggled. His little mouth gasped.

"Oh no!" I said. Then more urgently,

"OH NO!" If Pip was a tadpole, that meant he had gills now. He couldn't breathe unless he was underwater.

I looked left and then right and quickly spotted a puddle. That would work for now. I gently scooped the flopping Pip tadpole into it.

"Sassafras!" I called, and he came bounding over. I pointed to the puddle. "Pip is a tadpole now," I choked out. "Please watch him."

"Mrow," said Sassafras.

I ran to the barn, filled a big jar with

water, and rushed back to Sassafras. I fished around in the puddle, found Pip, and put him in the jar. He opened and closed his mouth like he was trying to talk, but I couldn't understand him anymore.

Wishy watched with her mouth wide open and tears pouring down her face. "Zoey, I am—*hic*—so sorry—*hic*—!"

I managed to squeak out, "It's OK. It was an accident," and then I ran into the barn with the jar to cry.

# CHAPTER 18
# THINKING GOGGLES

Sassafras tried to make me feel better by curling up in my lap and rubbing his face on my legs. But how could I feel better when two of my best friends were in so much trouble?

I took some deep breaths to calm down. I scratched Sassafras's chin. "Being upset doesn't help anyone think. Right, Sassafras?"

Sassafras sat up and meowed. Then he trotted off and returned with my Thinking

Goggles in his mouth.

"Oh, good boy. Yes, Thinking Goggles help me think. You're such a smart kitty." I gave him a squeeze, and he settled back into my lap.

I held my Thinking Goggles out in front of me. "If there was ever a time that I *really* needed your help, Thinking Goggles, this is *it*! Please, please help me!"

I put them on my head. And waited. And waited some more.

While waiting, I fidgeted with my sweater and plucked off a leaf. "That must have gotten stuck when we were wandering through the forest," I muttered to myself.

I fussed a little more with my sweater and found a patch of kitten fur. "Aw, I wonder how the kittens are doing," I said to myself. Thinking of the kittens made me remember how Sage liked having us rub her chin and pet her belly at the same time. I rubbed Sassafras's chin and belly at the same time, and he exploded with purrs.

My whole body seemed to rumble with his big purrs. Even my Thinking Goggles. "OH!" I stood up suddenly. Poor Sassafras tumbled to the floor and gave me a sour look. "Sorry, buddy! But I think that's it!" I grinned down at him. "Sage needed *two* things at once to make her purr. Maybe I need to try the two things that seemed to help Wishy's hiccups the most *at the same*

*time*!"

I flipped open my science journal to check my data chart and then gathered my supplies. I rushed over to Wishy and explained my plan. "Please, please work," I whispered.

Wishy swallowed the spoonful of peanut butter, and then grabbed the cup and drank the whole thing with the straw. She turned to me and said, "Do you think it worked this time, Zoey?"

We both stood there with our mouths open for a moment.

"Do you hear that? WE DID IT!" I shouted.

# CHAPTER 19
# PHOTO

After I'd rushed Wishy into the barn and she'd changed Pip back into Pip, we took tiny Tiny out into the yard and restored him to his normal size. Pip went back into the barn with me to convince the monster siblings that it was finally safe to come out. Wishy unstuck their hands, and we all cheered.

I looked around at everyone's smiling faces and got an idea. "Wait here, everyone!" I ran into the house and brought my mom and my camera outside. "Can I get a photo with everyone for my science journal?" I asked my friends.

Everyone nodded.

Pip raised a hand. "Wait one sec—we're just missing one thing."

He looked back at Wishy, and closed his eyes and smiled. Wishy nodded, and Pip's gorgeous green curls unfurled from his head at the same time his feet made a *whoomp* noise and grew several sizes.

"TINY, TOO!" said Tiny. He closed his eyes and zebra stripes appeared on his fur.

Pip grinned. "Now we're ready for the photo."

Tiny nodded his giant striped head.

Wishy floated over and put an arm around my left shoulder, and the monsters snuggled in on my right. Pip hopped up on my head, Sassafras leapt into my arms, and Tiny bent his head way, way down.

"Say cheese!" said Mom, and then a moment later, she handed me the photo.

"This is definitely one for the memory books."

"Exactly!" I said. "I'll be right back!"

I ran to my desk in my room, opened my science journal, and glued down the shimmering photo. Then I left it open to a new blank page, all ready for the next magical creature we would meet.

# GLOSSARY

**Data:** Information about your experiment that you write down. Data can be measurements or observations.

**Diaphragm:** A dome-shaped muscle that works to help you breathe in and out by getting tighter or looser.

**Gills:** The organ in fish and some amphibians that brings oxygen into their blood so they can "breathe."

**Lungs:** The organ in animals (other than fish and some reptiles) that brings oxygen into their blood so they can "breathe."

**Unconscious:** Like being asleep, but different. It can happen if you get very scared or very hurt.

# ABOUT THE AUTHOR
# AND ILLUSTRATOR

**ASIA CITRO** used to be a science teacher, but now she plays at home with her two kids and writes books. When she was little, she had a cat just like Sassafras. He loved to eat bugs and always made her laugh (his favorite toy was a plastic human nose that he carried everywhere). Asia has also written three activity books: *150+ Screen-Free Activities for Kids, The Curious Kid's Science Book,* and *A Little Bit of Dirt.* She has yet to find a baby dragon in her backyard, but she always keeps an eye out, just in case.

**MARION LINDSAY** is a children's book illustrator who loves stories and knows a good one when she reads it. She likes to draw anything and everything but does spend a completely unfair amount of time drawing cats. Sometimes she has to draw dogs just to make up for it. She illustrates picture books and chapter books as well as painting paintings and designing patterns. Like Asia, Marion is always on the lookout for dragons and sometimes thinks there might be a small one living in the airing cupboard.

for activities and more visit
ZOEYANDSASSAFRAS.COM